Ava & Gabby Danger

NINJA Princess DETECTIVES

HOT DIGGITY DOG GONE

by Kyla Steinkraus

Illustrated by Katie Wood

A Division of
Carson Dellosa Education

Rourke
Educational Media
rourkeeducationalmedia.com

© 2020 Rourke Educational Media

www.rourkeeducationalmedia.com

Edited by: *Kim Thompson*

Cover layout by: *Rhea Magaro-Wallace*

Interior layout by: *Kathy Walsh*

Cover and interior illustrations by: *Katie Wood*

Library of Congress PCN Data

Hot Diggity Dog Gone / Kyla Steinkraus
(Ava and Gabby Danger: Ninja Princess Detectives)
ISBN 978-1-73161-481-0 (hard cover) (alk. paper)
ISBN 978-1-73161-288-5 (soft cover)
ISBN 978-1-73161-586-2 (e-Book)
ISBN 978-1-73161-691-3 (ePub)

Library of Congress Control Number: 2019932318

Printed in the United States of America,
North Mankato, Minnesota

Dear Guardian/Educator,

Introduce your child to the wonderful world of reading with our leveled readers. Your growing reader will be continuously engaged as he or she is guided from one level to the next. Each level is carefully built to provide your child with the reading skills and knowledge to be a confident reader! Ultimately, we want your child to develop a love of reading.

Level 1 *Learning to Read*
High frequency words, basic sentences, large type, labels, full color illustrations to help young readers better comprehend the text

Level 2 *Beginning to Read Alone*
Short sentences, familiar words, simple plot, easy-to-read fonts

Level 3 *Reading on Your Own*
Short paragraphs, easy-to-follow plots, vocabulary is increasingly challenging, exciting stories

Level 4 *Proficient Reader*
Chapters, engaging stories, challenging vocabulary, multiple text features

Reading should be a pleasurable experience. A child who enjoys reading reads more, and a child who reads more becomes a better reader. Your child will grow with exposure to broad vocabulary and literary techniques, and will develop deeper critical thinking and comprehension skills. We are excited to be a part of your child's reading journey.

Happy reading,
Rourke Educational Media

Table of Contents

Chapter One

No Attitude for a Frog

"What a perfect day for a spring picnic!" Gabby Danger said.

"What a perfect day for a race!" her sister, Ava Danger, sang. "Come on!"

The sisters dashed across the drawbridge down to the palace lawn. Ava and Gabby were princesses. They were also ninjas-in-training. They lived in the palace at the top of the hill with their parents, the king and queen of the Kingdom of Klue.

Ava was older, with straight brown hair and glasses, while Gabby had short curly blonde hair that sprang up all over her head. They both loved dressing up in fancy princess gowns. They also loved working up a sweat in their martial arts classes.

Alex waved at them. "We've been waiting for you!"

"Happy Spring Picnic Day!" Gabby said as she and Ava sat down on a brightly colored blanket next to their friends.

"I'm so excited!" Mateo said around a big bite of hot dog.

The entire kingdom had turned out for the annual Klue Spring Picnic. Chef Pickles had grilled his best hot dogs with all the toppings. There were balloons and cotton candy—and LOTS of games and prizes.

The biggest event of all was the Hot Dog Race. But it wasn't just for dogs. All the pets

in the kingdom were invited to compete in the big race. The winner earned the title of Royal Pet for the entire year. They also got a year's supply of pet treats and a new gold collar. The pet's owner even won a thousand gold coins!

"I wonder who will win the race this year," Gabby said.

"That's the mystery!" Ava replied.

Ava and Gabby loved a good mystery. In fact, they were known around the Kingdom of Klue as the Ninja Princess Detectives. If anyone in the kingdom had a case to solve, they always came to the Danger girls.

"Who are the racers this year?" Gabby asked.

"I brought Max the Monkey," Mateo said. "He's up in a tree somewhere like always."

"Mr. Posh entered Paws the Cat, even though she refuses to run every single year."

Alex shook his head. "Cats!"

"Speaking of refusing to run," Ava said, "Did you see Slow Poke the Sloth? Miss Fix-It and Chef Pickles can't get him to wake up!"

Mateo laughed. "Or even move," he said.

Chef Pickles was the palace cook, and Miss Fix-It was the handywoman who fixed everything that broke in Klue. They shared Slow Poke, the slowest pet in the whole kingdom. They still entered him in the race every year. He usually fell asleep at the starting line.

Principal Knight, the principal of Dragon Elementary School, entered her fuzzy pink bunny. His name was Spike, the Fire-Breathing Rabbit. No one knew whether he really breathed fire. No one wanted to find out, either.

CoCo the Parrot perched on the shoulder of Sensei Suki, their martial arts instructor, as she played lawn darts with Mr. Posh, the palace housekeeper.

"Don't forget Erk," Ava said, "fastest hopper in the East!"

"We'll see," Gabby said. She didn't have high hopes for Erk.

"I heard that!" Erk croaked from inside Ava's pocket.

Erk was their pet frog. He could talk, but only the sisters could understand him. He'd taught them to speak Ribbit soon after he showed up in the palace. Ava and Gabby thought he might be a prince stuck in a frog body, like a frog in a fairy tale. But neither wanted to kiss him to find out. That was just gross.

"I really hope Freddy wins." Alex sounded sad. His shoulders slumped. He watched his ferret chase a yellow balloon. It matched his own yellow vest.

"Are you okay, Alex?" Ava asked.

"I really, really want a new remote-controlled race car," he said glumly. "Mine broke. But the only way I can buy one is if I win the thousand gold coins."

"Good luck!" Ava called as Alex ran off after Freddy.

"Pepper will win for sure," Ella said.

"Definitely," Bella said.

Daniella clapped her hands. "She's even faster than Bolt!"

Gabby gasped. "Really?"

Pepper was the triplets' prize puppy. Pepper's dad was named Bolt because he was as fast as a lightning bolt. Bolt had won the last seven races in a row. Now it was Pepper's turn.

"No way," Jade said as she walked up. She

pointed proudly at the snowy white unicorn galloping near the pond. "Sparkles is faster than last year. We've been practicing in the corral day and night."

"That's too much practicing," Mateo said with a grin. "When do you sleep?"

"We'll do anything to win!" Jade said. She was smart and great at martial arts. There was no doubt she would join the ranks of Klue's greatest ninjas one day. And she liked to win just as much as Ava did.

Bella put her hands on her hips. "Pepper is going to win, no contest!"

"Where is Pepper, anyway?" Gabby asked. She hadn't seen the puppy all day.

"She kept chasing her tail," Daniella said.

"We had to leash her to a tree," Bella said, "so she wouldn't run away."

"She just wanted to play," Ella said sadly.

"Prize-winning pups don't have time to play," Bella reminded her.

Ella's shoulders rose as she took a deep breath. Then she sighed dramatically, her shoulders dropping.

"The annual Hot Dog Race begins in an hour!" Mr. Posh announced, clapping his hands loudly over his head. "It's officially time to warm up our racers!"

Everyone ran to get their pets. Miss Fix-It and Chef Pickles tried to wake up Slow Poke. The sloth just snored louder.

Mateo coaxed Max the Monkey down from his favorite tree. Jade and Sparkles the Unicorn galloped around the pond as fast as they could. And Ella, Bella, and Daniella went to get Pepper.

Ava pulled Erk out of her pocket and laid

him gently on the grass. "Come on, Erk. Your turn."

Erk flopped onto his belly. "Too hot."

"That's no attitude for a frog!" said Ava. Her competitive side was kicking in. She especially wanted to beat Jade.

Erk pressed his little green arm to his little green head. He gasped. He sweated. He gasped again.

Gabby pulled a leaf from a nearby tree and fanned him.

"Much better," Erk croaked.

"Show us your fastest hop," Gabby said.

He only shook his head.

"Come on, Erk!" Ava begged. "You're a frog! Hop!"

"Rather have a nap," he croaked.

"This is hopeless!" Ava sighed.

Suddenly, someone screamed.

Chapter Two

Vanished

Everyone ran to the edge of the woods, the king and queen leading the group. Ella, Bella, and Daniella stood around the tree where Pepper had been tied up. The purple leash was still there. So was the collar. But there was no puppy inside it.

"Pepper is missing!" Bella cried.

"Do you think she ran away?" Daniella asked.

Gabby knelt carefully in the grass. "If Pepper had slipped out of her collar, it would still be buckled. If she chewed through it, there would be bite marks." She picked up the collar for everyone to see. "But this collar is in perfect shape."

Mr. Posh gasped. "That means..."

"Someone stole Pepper!" Gabby said.

"Who would steal a puppy?" Bella wailed.

"Someone who wanted to win the race themselves," Ava said. "We have a real mystery on our hands!"

"Ava and Gabby, can you search for clues while we look for the puppy?" Mom asked. "We need to find her before the race starts."

Gabby nodded. "Don't worry! We're on the case!"

Mom, Dad, Mr. Posh, Principal Knight, and the rest of the grown-ups spread out, yelling "Pepper! PEPPER!" as they searched the woods around the palace.

Bella turned to Ava and Gabby. Her eyes were red and full of tears. "Please find Pepper."

"Pretty please!" Daniella said.

"Don't worry," Ava said. "We'll save your pup. The ninja princess detectives always catch the culprit!"

Ella didn't say anything. She just hugged herself sadly. She usually talked the most of the talkative triplets. She seemed especially worried about Pepper.

Ava and Gabby weren't worried, though. They knew they could find the missing pup!

"Time to put on our thinking crowns!" they said together.

With the golden crowns on their heads, they could solve any case.

"The first thing we need to do is study

the scene of the crime." Gabby took out her magnifying glass covered in sparkling jewels. She examined the collar again. No bite marks. No tears. No clues.

Ava studied the ground around the tree. The grass was bent where Pepper had rested. There was a bare patch of dirt near the trunk of the tree.

Ava knelt down next to it. She saw something. "A footprint!"

"How big is it?" Gabby asked.

Ava lined up her foot next to the footprint. They matched almost perfectly. "The same size as my foot."

"So the thief is a kid our age," Gabby said.

"Yes!" Ava said. "Our first clue!"

"That's, um, not from the thief," Ella said quietly.

"What do you mean?" Gabby asked.

Ella's cheeks turned red. "That was me."

"When?" Ava asked.

"Right before we ate the hot dogs. I came back to give Pepper a scratch and a treat," Ella admitted.

"She's not supposed to have treats before the race," Daniella said.

Ella hung her head. "I couldn't help it."

"So we have no clues after all," Gabby huffed, disappointed.

"Wait!" Something bright caught Ava's eye. It was almost hidden in the grass, but she still noticed it. Detectives notice everything.

She bent and picked up the object. It was a small yellow button. "This could have fallen off when the culprit took the puppy!"

Gabby took out her pink, sparkly notebook

and fluffy unicorn pen. She opened the notebook to a blank page and wrote **Clues** neatly across the top. On another page, she wrote **Suspects.**

Ava scanned the picnic area. She tried to remember what everyone was wearing. A yellow balloon sailed into the air above the trees. "Alex! The balloon Freddy the Ferret was chasing matched Alex's vest. It had buttons on the front too!"

Gabby wrote **Alex** on the list of suspects. "He really wanted to win so he could buy that remote-controlled race car."

"How much does he want to win?" Ava asked. "Enough to steal a puppy?"

"Let's find out!" Gabby said. "Time to observe our first suspect. Maybe we can catch him with Pepper."

Chapter Three

Everyone's a Suspect

A va and Gabby darted from tree to tree near the edge of the woods, keeping an eye out for Alex. Their steps were silent as they tried to blend into the surroundings. A good ninja can see without being seen, and they were good ninjas. When they spotted Alex, he had a dog, all right! But it wasn't Pepper. It was one of Chef Pickles's hot dogs.

Principal Knight was sitting next to Alex. She was busy eating a hot dog too. Freddy the Ferret slept in Alex's lap. The bottom button of his vest was missing.

Ava's heart beat faster. Were they about to solve the case already? That would be a record-breaker!

"May we ask you a few questions, Alex?" Gabby asked.

Alex looked around, then nodded glumly.

"Did you see Pepper today?"

Alex shook his head. "I didn't take her, I promise!"

"We know how much you want to win," Gabby said.

"Not that much! I would never take someone's pet!"

Ava held up the yellow button. "Are you sure?"

Alex's eyes widened.

"I believe that belongs to you," Gabby said. "Time to admit the truth!"

Alex looked at Principal Knight. She gave him a nod. "Go ahead."

"Okay," he sighed. "I was chasing after Freddy, and he ran over to Pepper. The puppy seemed lonely. So I played with her for a few minutes. She must have torn off the button when she jumped on me."

"Likely story!" Erk croaked from his perch on Ava's shoulder.

Gabby tapped her chin with her fluffy pen. "Did anyone see you?"

Alex looked like he might cry. "No, I don't think so."

"So you don't have an alibi," Ava said.

"I don't even know what that is!" Alex said.

"An alibi means you can prove you weren't at the scene at the time of the crime," Gabby explained.

Principal Knight took a bite of her hot dog. "I can give Alex an alibi."

Ava raised her eyebrows. "You can?"

"I checked on Pepper right before Mr. Posh made his announcement that it was time to warm up for the race. Then I sat on this bench to enjoy my hot dog. Alex couldn't get Freddy to do anything but chase that balloon, so he came and sat next to me. He was with me when the triplets started screaming."

"So he can't be the culprit," Gabby said.

"You're in the clear, Alex," Ava said.

"Thanks," Alex mumbled.

"Why didn't you tell us the truth?" Gabby asked.

Alex looked down at Freddy in his lap. "I was scared you wouldn't believe me."

Gabby crossed Alex's name off her list of suspects. "Did you see anything suspicious?"

"No." Alex shook his head. "But I might have heard something."

"What?" Ava and Gabby asked together.

"After we found out Pepper was missing, Jade walked past me," Alex said. "I heard her say, 'That dog should stay missing.'"

"Hmm," Gabby said.

"That sounds very suspicious," Ava said.

"Very suspicious, indeed," Erk croaked.

"Exactly." Gabby scribbled fiercely in her notebook. "Thanks, Alex. You were a big help."

Ava and Gabby left a relieved Alex happily petting Freddy while Principal Knight finished her food. They snuck back toward the pond, trying to blend in so they could observe Jade in secret, ninja-style.

They spotted Jade and Sparkles practicing for the race. But Jade had spotted them too. She was good.

"I didn't take that puppy," Jade called out without looking in their direction.

"Feeling guilty?" Ava asked, emerging from their hiding spot.

"Anything you want to confess?" Gabby added.

"Wanting to win isn't a crime." Jade looked straight at Ava. "Is it?"

"No," Ava admitted. She liked winning too.

"It is if you cheat," Gabby said.

"You said you were willing to do anything to win, remember?" Ava asked.

"That's a motive, a possible reason for committing a crime," Gabby explained.

Jade put her hands on her hips. "I meant 'anything' like practicing instead of playing. And getting up early instead of sleeping in."

That made sense to Ava. But Gabby still looked suspicious.

Sparkles pushed her nose against Jade's shoulder. She neighed, eager to get back to practicing. "Do you have any actual evidence?" Jade asked.

"No," Gabby admitted.

Ava frowned. Another suspect crossed off the list. They needed another clue!

"Did you see anything between Mr. Posh's announcement and when the triplets discovered Pepper was missing?" Gabby asked.

"Nothing." Jade shrugged. "Well, just Miss Fix-It carting trash cans across the lawn."

"Why was that strange?" Gabby asked. Miss Fix-It emptied trash cans into the dumpster in the back of the palace all the time.

"From what I could see, they looked empty. It's strange that she would take empty trash cans to the dumpster."

That did seem odd. Ava and Gabby looked at each other. It was worth investigating.

"I'm sorry I couldn't help." Jade rubbed Sparkles's nose. "I really do hope Pepper is all right."

"It's okay," Gabby said. "Sometimes a wrong clue leads us to the right one!"

Chapter Four

Crooks!

Ava and Gabby dashed across the palace lawn toward the hot dog grill. "Miss Fix-It could have hidden the puppy inside the trash can!"

"No one would think to look inside," Gabby said. "That's how she stole Pepper away without anyone seeing!"

"But why would she want to take Pepper?" Ava asked. "What's her motive?"

Gabby tapped her fuzzy pen on her chin. "That's what we need to find out."

Miss Fix-It stood beside Chef Pickles at the grill. Their backs were turned to the sisters. Their heads were bent as they whispered to each other.

Ava's ears perked up. Whenever anyone whispered, it was because they wanted to keep something a secret. A secret might be a clue!

Ava poked Gabby's arm and nodded with her chin, one of their secret signals that meant: Possible clue ahead! Ninjas always used secret signals to communicate.

They snuck a few silent steps closer so they could hear the whispers without being detected.

"...the triplets have beaten us one too many times," Miss Fix-It was saying. "First with Bolt and now this puppy."

"But this year we have our secret weapon," Chef Pickles whispered.

"It's time for a new Royal Pet!" Miss Fix-It said with certainty.

"Aha!" Ava cried. She couldn't help it. She couldn't stay quiet any longer. "You two are the crooks!"

Miss Fix-It and Chef Pickles spun around.

"Your secret weapon!" Ava said. "That's why you stole Pepper!"

"We do have a secret weapon," Miss Fix-It said, "but it's not what you think. It's Slow Poke."

Ava frowned, confused. "Your sloth?"

"We would never steal a cute little puppy," Chef Pickles said.

"Hmm," Gabby said, thinking hard. "Then what about the strangely empty trash cans?"

Miss Fix-It smiled. "The king asked me to put some empty trash cans next to the race course so people could easily throw their trash away."

"Oh," Gabby said.

"Oops," Ava said.

"Five minutes until race time!" Mr. Posh announced.

"Hurry and solve the case!" Chef Pickles put down his spatula. "We're counting on you, princesses."

They were running out of time! Ava turned to her sister and adjusted her thinking crown. "This doesn't make sense."

"I know." Gabby looked down at her notebook. "The only clue we still have is the footprint beside Pepper's leash."

"But Ella admitted it was hers right away," Ava said.

"Hmm," Gabby said.

Suddenly, Ava had a feeling in her gut. It was her ninja instincts. She felt it, then she knew. She looked at Gabby. Gabby looked at her. Both girls' eyes widened.

"It's her!" Gabby said.

"Yes!" Ava replied.

They'd figured out the mystery at the same time!

Ava grinned. "Should we pay the crime scene another visit?"

Gabby grinned right back. "We should!"

"I don't get it," Erk croaked.

"We are following a hunch!" Gabby said.

"We're following our ninja guts!" Ava added as they ran across the palace lawn.

The triplets were still sitting against the

tree, waiting for Pepper to come back. Bella held Pepper's collar. Daniella held her leash. They were both crying.

"Did you find her?" Bella cried.

"Is she safe?" Daniella asked.

"We don't know where she is yet," Gabby said. "But we know someone who does."

Ava and Gabby looked at Ella.

"I wondered if you would figure it out," Ella said quietly.

"Huh?" Bella said.

Daniella's mouth fell open. "What?"

"Go ahead, Ella," Ava said gently. "You should tell them."

Ella took a deep breath. "I took Pepper."

"What?" the two girls gasped.

"I—I didn't know what to do. I took her and

put her in our carriage. I was going to keep her there until the race was over."

"But why?" Bella asked.

"You didn't want Pepper to race," Gabby guessed.

"That's why you've been so quiet and sad," Ava reasoned.

Ella wiped away a tear and nodded. "Every time I tried to play with her, everyone said she had to practice racing. I don't want her to be a prize racer! I don't care if she wins. I just want her to play and have fun ... as our pet!"

"Me too!" Bella said.

"Me three," Daniella whispered.

The triplets giggled and hugged each other.

"Case solved!" Ava said happily. "Just in time for the race!"

Chapter Five

Ready, Set, Race!

"**R**eady, set," Mom yelled from the starting line.

Dad stood at the finish-line ribbon. He held a giant jar of Chef Pickles's gourmet pet treats for the winner. Everyone crowded along the edges of the course to watch.

Beside them, Ella held Pepper. The puppy wiggled and licked Ella's smiling face.

"Go!" Dad yelled.

The pets took off! Sparkles the Unicorn galloped to an early lead. CoCo the Parrot flew above the other racers. Freddy the Ferret was fast, but he kept stopping to sniff every pine cone.

Slow Poke the Sloth yawned sleepily. He was still at the starting line. Paws the Cat walked slowly around the moat, her tail and her whiskered nose in the air. Spike the Rabbit hopped past her, not breathing fire after all. Max the Monkey dropped from the trees and scampered after Sparkles.

"Ladies and gentlemen, it's a close race!" Dad boomed. The pets ran across the drawbridge toward the finish line. Sparkles and Max raced neck and neck, even though the monkey only reached the unicorn's knees.

Suddenly a speeding blur overtook everyone, including Sparkles. The blur burst across the finish line first, breaking the ribbon.

"What was that?" Gabby asked in surprise.

Even Dad looked shocked. "Ah ... looks like Slow Poke wins!"

Chef Pickles and Miss Fix-It jumped up and down in excitement. "Way to go, Slow Poke!" Slow Poke grabbed the jar of pet treats and gobbled them up in one gulp.

Ava gave a big cheer for Slow Poke. She did love to win, but a princess always loses gracefully. Erk hadn't even bothered to hop across the finish line before returning to Ava's pocket. He wasn't the fastest jumper in the East after all. That was okay. The ninja princess detectives liked him just the way he was.

Ella laughed as Pepper licked her nose. "That was a surprise! How can a sloth move that quickly?"

"Hmm," Gabby said.

"Smells like another mystery!" Ava sang. She patted Erk's small green head. "What could be more fun than that?"

Ninja Basics

In ancient Japan, ninjas were expert warriors and spies. They were trained in martial arts from a young age. They learned to fight, but they preferred to use stealth.

Ninjas wore dark clothes so they could hide in the dark. They wore special socks instead of shoes to sneak around quietly. They also had metal claws they put on their feet to climb the walls of tall buildings.

Some people thought ninjas had magical powers. They believed ninjas could fly and even walk on water. While they weren't magical, ninjas were strong, skilled, patient, and smart problem-solvers!

Super Ninja Skills You Can Use

Focus

An important thinking skill, focus, helps ninjas put all their attention and effort into completing a task. They use their sharp mental abilities to block out distractions as they work. Next time you're doing homework, pay attention to everything that distracts you. Then, try shifting into ninja mode. Block out the distractions until your homework mission is complete!

Stealth

Ninjas have a reputation for their silent movements. They can sneak almost anywhere without a sound! This helps them travel undetected in dangerous areas. Listen to the noises you normally make as you walk around your house or classroom. Then try walking silently like a ninja. Where could you use this stealth ninja skill?

Writing Mysteries

Mysteries are a genre, or category, of literature that focus on solving a mysterious problem, crime, or situation. A mystery has five basic elements:

1. **The mystery**! A pet goes missing. A favorite toy is stolen. Something strange happens, and no one knows why.

2. **The detective(s)**. The detective is the character who investigates the situation, interviews witnesses, and eventually solves the case.

3. **Clues**. Clues are evidence that help lead the detective to the solution. And then there are red herrings! A red herring is a fake clue that authors put in a mystery to throw the detective (and the reader!) off the right track.

4. **The suspect(s)**. Every good mystery has at least one suspect, or person the detective thinks is responsible. Two or three suspects makes it harder to solve the case. The detective must collect evidence to prove the suspect is guilty.

5. **The solution!** Solving the case is the best part of every mystery. The detective puts all the clues together and figures out the answer to the puzzle. The real clues need to make sense and help the detective crack the case.

Try It!

Ask a friend or family member to give you a person's name, an object, and a place. Now you have a character, a stolen object, and a setting! Write a mystery story based on these prompts.

Race for the Trophy!

Gather your supplies and follow the directions to make a trophy worthy of a racing champion!

Supplies

- the cardboard cylinder from a roll of toilet paper
- an old CD or a small paper plate
- tape
- a paper or plastic cup
- aluminum foil
- paper
- markers or colored pencils

Directions

1. Tape the cardboard roll onto the old CD (or paper plate). If you have trouble getting it to stick, make a few cuts to the edge of the roll to squish it flat.

2. Tape the bottom of the cup to the other side of the roll.

3. It's time to make your trophy shine. Roll out the aluminum foil. Wrap your creation carefully in foil and mold it until it is completely covered.

4. Use markers or colored pencils to draw a label on paper. Tape it onto your trophy.

5. Fill your trophy cup with candy or other treats.

6. Race! You might set up an obstacle course race, a relay race, or a timed race. Try these ideas for moving like an animal as you race:

   • Hop like a frog.

   • Walk on all fours like a cat.

   • Gallop like a unicorn.

   • Hold your ankles and scamper like a monkey.

   • Move very slowly like a sloth (the slowest one wins!).

7. Award the trophy to the winner. Race again in a day or two, passing the trophy to the new winner each time.

About the Author

Kyla Steinkraus has been writing stories since she was five years old. Before she could write, she told stories into a recorder. Her parents still have some of them! Kyla lives with her two kids, her husband, and two very spoiled cats in Atlanta, Georgia. When she's not writing, Kyla loves hiking in the mountains, reading awesome books, and playing board games with her family. She has been known to jump out of a plane occasionally—parachute included, of course!

About the Illustrator

Katie Wood has loved drawing since she was very small, which inspired her to study illustration at Loughborough University. She now feels extremely lucky to be drawing every day from her studio in Leicester, England. She is never happier than when she is drawing with a cup of tea, or walking in the countryside with her unhelpful studio assistant, Inka the dog.